BAZ & BENZ

Heidi McKinnon

SIMON & SCHUSTER BOOKS FOR YOUNG READERS
An imprint of Simon & Schuster Children's Publishing Division
1230 Avenue of the Americas, New York, New York 10020
Copyright © 2019 by Heidi McKinnon
Originally published in Australia in 2019 by Allen & Unwin.
All rights reserved, including the right of reproduction in whole or in part in any form.

W9-CPX-582

Benz, are we friends?

Yes, Baz, we are bestest friends.

For how long?

Forever and ever.

What if I turned purple?

That would be funny!
But I would still be your friend.

What if I turned purple
and had spots?

That would be REALLY funny!

What if I said MEEP
all the time?

That would be annoying.

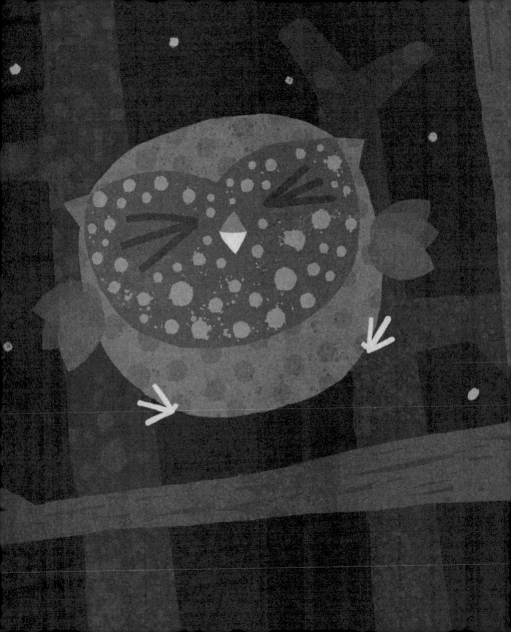

Meep!

MeeP! Meep!

mmeeeEEP!

MEEP! MEEP! MEEP!

MEEP!

That would be

reaLLy

annOying!

MEEP!

Stop.

What if I disappeared?

Then I would be sad
and miss you a lot.

But I would still be your friend . . .

Forever and ever.

Because you are you.

Meep!